Lady Lupin's Book of Etiquette

Babette Cole

For Lady Lupin Longtail
(Royal Dog of Scotland)
and
her lovely puppies

Published by
PEACHTREE PUBLISHERS
1700 Chattahoochee Avenue
Atlanta, Georgia 30318-2112

www.peachtree-online.com

Text and Illustrations © 2002 by Babette Cole.

First published by Penguin Books Ltd. for Hamish Hamilton Ltd. in 2001

First United States edition published by Peachtree Publishers in 2002

10 9 8 7 6 5 4 3 2 1
First Edition

Set in Monotype Baskerville

Printed in Italy by L.E.G.O.

ISBN 1-56145-257-2

United States Library of Congress Cataloging-in-Publication Number 2001005336

Lady Lupin's Book of Etiquette

Babette Cole

Ω
PEACHTREE
ATLANTA

"Now that you are growing
up," said Lady Lupin
to her puppies,

"it is time to learn about
ETIQUETTE."

"What does that mean, dear Mother?" asked Lady Lobelia.

"How to behave like ladies and gentledogs so that everyone will love you," said Lady Lupin.

"It may even help you
to get a good
mate!"

"For instance, do not squabble
over your bones.

Instead, ask each other politely,
'Please pass the bones,
dear Brother.'

'Of course,
Lobelia.'

'Thank you so much,
Luchie!'

At dinner, never serve yourself first.

← side plate and butter knife

dessert spoon

and fork

DINNER PLATE

glass

This is how your place is set.

MEAT

FISH

1 : COURSE

SOUP

Oysters are
eaten raw
from the
shell...

with lemon juice.

Spaghetti is eaten
with a fork
only.

Use a spike and tongs
for snails.

You need a shell cracker
to eat lobster.

Never bark with your mouth full!

Or leave the
table …

without asking permission!

Try not to show off at parties!

woof   woof   woof   woof   woof   woof   woof   woof

Always send thank-you letters.

Longtail Castle
Lochbone
Scotland

Lady Snoutover
Pedigree Park
Pawshire

Sept. 20, 2001

Dear Lady Snoutover,
    Thank you so much for your party
last Saturday. I enjoyed it
enormously.
Yours sincerely,
Lady Lobelia Longtail

Never ask an older lady her age!

Remember that ladies always go first!

Messy eaters
should avoid hats with veils.

Shake paws correctly.

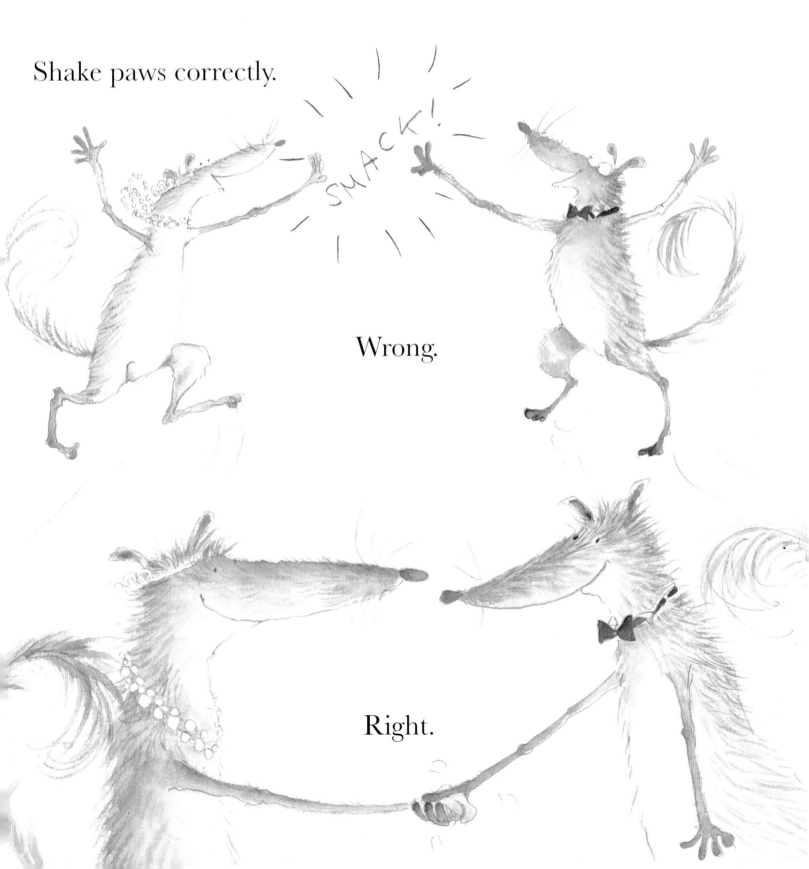

SMACK!

Wrong.

Right.

Remember to open doors for older dogs.

And offer them a seat!

It's easier to say
you're sorry
in writing.

Longtail Castle
Loch Fone
Scotland

The Earl of Earwig
Fleas Castle
Great Itchington
Sussex

Sept 21, 2001

Dear Lord Earwig,

I really am most awfully sorry
for causing your fall at Longtail
Castle yesterday. Please accept
my apologies.

Yours very sincerely
Lady Lobelia
Longtail

A neat appearance can be attractive.

Brushed snout,

clean nails.

Too much makeup may give an
unsuitable impression…

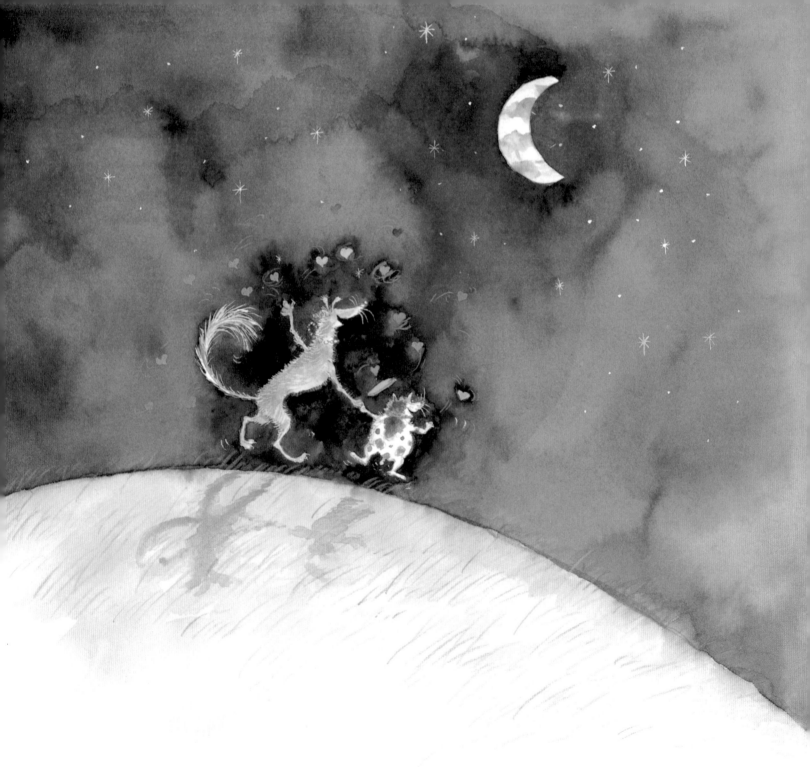

and could attract the wrong mate!

And above all, remain calm when
faced with the
unexpected!"

Born in England, Babette Cole graduated from Canterbury College of Art in 1973, and she has been a writer and an illustrator ever since.

Babette lives on a farm in eastern England with two Norfolk terriers and three Scottish deerhounds, including the ones that appear in this story—Lady Lupin, Lobelia, and Luciano.

Babette has written and illustrated numerous other books, including THE BAD GOOD MANNERS BOOK, PRINCESS SMARTYPANTS, DR. DOG, and PRINCE CINDERS. Babette says she does not set out to make her books unconventional—"They just happen that way!"